We Wonder What Will Walter Be?

When He Grows Up

by Crockett Johnson

Holt, Rinehart and Winston

New York   Chicago   San Francisco

WALTER wished somebody could decide for him. He was trying to think what to be when he grew up.

While he wondered about it, he strolled around in the early sunshine, here and there and this way and that, and he found himself in a wilderness.

It was there he met the Lion.

"You seem to have a problem," said the Lion.
"I can't think what to grow up to be," said Walter.
The Lion showed considerable interest.
"Have you a choice?" he said.
"I will have a choice," said Walter, "as soon as I can think what to decide."

"Such a decision certainly needs a lot of careful thought," said the Lion. "I'll summon the members of my council."

"Who are they?" said Walter.

"The best thinkers in the kingdom," said the Lion. "I've chosen them from among the brightest thinkers,

the hardest thinkers, the deepest thinkers, thinkers of
the biggest thoughts, thinkers of the highest thoughts,
the fastest thinkers . . ."

"Good," said Walter. "I was hoping that somebody
could decide for me. It's a difficult problem."

"Don't give it another thought," said the Lion.

He threw back his head and his loud roar went out across the wilderness.

"A strange young one here says he can choose what to grow up to be! But he can't make up his mind!"

Almost immediately a small cloud of dust arose in the distance.

The cloud of dust grew rapidly as it approached
Walter and the Lion.

An animal raced toward them, flying along the
ground with lengthy leaps and bounds.

It went by with a clatter of hooves.

And it kept right on going.

"Sure," said the Lion. "He's our fastest thinker."

"He is?" said Walter.

"We had a foot race to prove it," said the Lion.

Walter watched the Antelope bound away in his cloud of dust. He watched the dust cloud grow tiny and disappear over the hills.

"That's the Antelope," said the Lion.
"He certainly can run fast," said Walter.
The Lion nodded.
"Speediest member of my council," he said.
"Is he going to think about what I should be when I grow up?" said Walter.

"I guess he was going so fast he couldn't think to stop," said Walter. "When will he stop and think?"

The Lion had turned his attention elsewhere, to a small hole in the ground near a clump of grass.

"Don't worry over the Antelope," he said. "He's always first to arrive at the answer. You'll see."

There was nothing to see of the Antelope. He was entirely out of sight. Walter joined the Lion who was peering into the hole.

Out of the hole came two little paws and a small head with a pointed snoot.

"A council member," said the Lion. "The Mole."

The Mole thrust its head to and fro and then waved it around and around in a blind circle.

"He's about to go back to the bottom of his tunnel and think about your problem," said the Lion.

"Him?" said Walter.

"Why not?" said the Lion.

Walter waited until the Mole, after revolving its head a few more times, crawled back down into the darkness of the earth. Then he answered the Lion.

"Well," he said, "for one thing, he doesn't look very bright, does he?"

"No," said the Lion, "he doesn't."

He turned away. Walter remained, staring down at the empty opening in the ground.

"Appearances deceive, don't they?" said the Lion. "It was some time before I realized the Mole was our deepest thinker. But here comes somebody you'll say looks bright enough—the Flamingo."

A flaming red bird with legs like sticks and a long rubbery neck came up and blinked foolishly at Walter.

Walter blinked back at the Flamingo.

"A brilliant council member," said the Lion.

He strode off, leaving Walter to stare at the bird's dazzling feathers.

"I didn't mean this kind of bright," said Walter. "I meant a way of thinking."

"There are many ways of thinking," said the Lion, "and we want to consider this problem of yours from all angles, don't we?"

"I guess so," said Walter.

"High thinking, for instance," said the Lion. "I can't imagine deciding so serious a question without a goodly amount of highly elevated thought, can you?"

"What?" said Walter.

He turned away from the Flamingo.

And next to the Lion he saw four tall legs beneath

a spotted body. His eyes ran up an enormously long, stiff neck to a head with short horns on it and a face that peered distantly down on everything.

"Oh," said Walter.

"The Giraffe," said the Lion. "I was referring to the Giraffe, of course."

The Giraffe took his place at the council, looking down his nose at Walter.

The Lion went on talking.

"Yes," he said, "we need every sort of thinking. We need high thoughts, and we need . . ."

He paused.

The earth had begun to shake under a tremendous thumping. As the pounding came closer, the Lion had to raise his voice to be heard.

"And we need big thoughts!"

Walter watched the Elephant arrive.

"Oh," he said.

The Elephant glanced at Walter and went over to the Giraffe and the Flamingo near the Mole's hole, and the Lion resumed his speech.

"But, perhaps most of all, do you know what this problem needs?"

Before anybody else could reply, he answered.

"It needs plenty of plain old hard thinking," he said. "That's what."

At that moment Walter spied what seemed to be a flat rock moving in to join them.

He tugged at the Lion's tail.

"Look," he said.

"Ah, yes!" said the Lion. "The Turtle. Now the council is complete."

He sat down near the moving rock that now quite plainly had four feet and a neck and head.

Walter stared at it and the Turtle looked back up at him with sleepy eyes. Walter shook his head.

"He doesn't seem even as bright as the Mole," he said. "He looks as if he can hardly think at all."

The Lion tapped the back of his paw against the Turtle's rocklike shell.

"Hardly think?" he said. "Yes, without doubt, he is our hardest thinker."

The Turtle's eyes closed all the way and his head went slowly back into the shell.

Walter continued to stare at the shell.

Strangely, as time went by, it began to seem that the Turtle inside might very well be thinking hard.

The animals all seemed wrapped in silent thought.

Now and then the Elephant shifted his huge weight
with a heavy sigh, as though he were pondering one
ponderous thought after another.

The Giraffe paced slowly from place to place, his
head rigid on his long neck, giving the impression of
pursuing lofty thoughts in a high-minded manner.

The sun rose higher in the fair sky. The Flamingo, who no longer was blinking foolishly but had his eyes shut tight, looked very bright indeed in the glare.

The hole in the sod was a reminder of the Mole. It was easy to picture the tiny creature down there in his burrow, thinking deeply beneath the ground.

"Hasn't there been enough thinking?" said Walter.
"Yes," said the Lion. "Where is that Antelope?"
"Do we have to wait for him?" said Walter.
"We always wait for the Antelope," said the Lion.
"If he wasn't always first with the answer, he wouldn't
be our fastest thinker, would he?"

The sun had not moved much higher when, over the distant hills, came the sound of hooves.

Walter saw a cloud of dust approaching.

The animals stirred expectantly.

The Elephant shifted his feet and swished his trunk.

The Giraffe peered along his nose at the dust cloud.

The Flamingo straightened his rubbery neck.
The Mole popped up in his hole.
The Turtle's head slid halfway out of his shell.
The Lion stepped forward impatiently.
So did Walter.
The Antelope raced toward them.

He arrived with a bound and skidded to a stop.
Panting, he faced Walter.
"I thought it all out at top speed!" he said.
"Good," said Walter.
The Antelope was almost completely breathless.
"I have the answer!" he said.

"Out with it!" said the Lion.

The Antelope excitedly fixed his eyes on Walter.

"You know what you ought to be when you grow up?" he said. "Do you know what?"

"What?" said Walter.

"An Antelope!" said the Antelope.

Before a suitable reply occurred to Walter, a small voice came to him from the ground near his feet.

"I've thought about it deeply."

"Yes?" said Walter.

"Be a Mole!" said the Mole.

"Be a Flamingo!" said the Flamingo.

Another voice came from high in the air, so quiet and so aloof that it scarcely could be heard. Walter looked up at the Giraffe.

"Be a Giraffe!" said the Giraffe.

It appeared at the moment that, of all the animals, only the Lion had nothing to say.

Walter edged away and the Lion accompanied him, looking apologetic.

A trumpet sounded. Walter turned in the direction of the blast.

"Be an Elephant!" said the Elephant.

The Turtle stretched his neck out of the shell. His

head searched from side to side until he managed to
focus his eyes on Walter.

"Be a Turtle!" said the Turtle.

Walter backed off. With a polite nod to all the
animals, he turned to leave.

"Thank you," he said.

The Lion padded along with Walter for a short way. "So many different answers!" he said.

"But they all had the same answer, really," said Walter. "Each one thought I ought to be like him."

"I don't understand it," said the Lion. "No, there must have been something wrong with the question."

"I have to go now," said Walter.

"One last thought," said the Lion. "Whatever you decide, be sure to make your decision bravely, without fear. Think boldly!"

"I will," said Walter.

"Yes!" said the Lion. "And grow up to be a Lion!"

Walter went on alone, with the sun high in the sky, on a path that seemed to lead directly out of the wilderness. As he walked along, he thought.

He still didn't know what to be when he grew up. But now he was sure he would be able to think about it and decide better than anybody else.

Crockett Johnson, unlike Walter, the hero of his story, was never really faced with the perplexity of deciding what he would be when he grew up, for he has become successful in several fields—most particularly as the prominent author-illustrator of over two dozen books for children.

Widely popular for his HAROLD stories, Mr. Johnson was for ten years the creator of *Barnaby,* a nationally syndicated comic strip which has been published as books, made into a play, and was recently adapted for television. In addition, he has worked as a typographer and art editor in the magazine field.

Mr. Johnson, who studied art at New York University and Cooper Union, grew up on the north shore of Long Island. He and his wife, Ruth Krauss, a poet and also a distinguished author of books for young people, now reside in Fairfield County, Connecticut.